Positive Thoughts

Living Your Life to the Fullest

POSITIVE THOUGHTS

Living Your Life to the Fullest

Ariel Books

♦

Andrews McMeel Publishing

Kansas City

Positive Thoughts: Living Your Life to the Fullest copyright © 1995, 2001 by Armand Eisen. All rights reserved. Printed in Singapore. No part of this book may be used or reproduced in any manner whatsoever without written permission except in the case of reprints in the context of reviews. For information, write Andrews McMeel Publishing, an Andrews McMeel Universal company, 4520 Main Street, Kansas City, Missouri 64111.

ISBN: 0-7407-1943-2

Library of Congress Catalog Card Number: 2001089271

Contents

Introduction • 7

Part I:
Optimism Begins with You • *11*

Part II:
The Positive Perspective • *213*

Introduction

OPTIMISM. What is this state of mind that everyone is always talking about? Doctors claim it helps people recover more quickly from illnesses. Executives encourage their salespeople to practice it. Many people repeatedly intone positive affirmations to help them achieve their goals. Whether learning to water ski or asking for a raise, we've all experienced the benefit of a positive attitude.

Looking on the bright side of things is a strategy that has been used for centuries. Is the glass half empty or half full? Becoming an optimist is a personal decision and one that has profound ramifications on how we see the world. If we think positively about ourselves, about others, and about the world around us, the world often meets our expectations.

Optimistic people tend to achieve their personal and professional goals. Think of someone you know who seems to be getting what he wants out of life. Chances are this person feels good about himself, thinks the world is a nice place, and has more friends than enemies.

How does one become an optimist? It takes

practice. The great thing about cultivating a positive outlook is that you can practice all day long without taking any extra time out of your schedule. So, the next time you're challenged, try telling yourself, "I can do it . . . I will do a great job." Before you know it, you'll be feeling more confident, more capable. The world will become sunnier and friendlier. And *you'll* be happier.

Part I

Optimism Begins with You

> *Keep your face to the sunshine and you cannot see the shadow.*

Helen Keller

Change your thoughts and you change your world.

— NORMAN VINCENT PEALE

Storybook happiness involves every form of pleasant thumb twiddling; true happiness involves the full use of one's powers and talents.

John W. Gardner

It was on my fifth birthday
that Papa put his hand on my shoulder
and said, "Remember, my son,
if you ever need a helping hand,
you'll find one at the end of your arm."

— *Sam Levenson* —

Seek not good from without: seek it within yourselves, or you will never find it.

EPICTETUS

*To live exhilaratingly
in and for the moment is
deadly serious work, fun of
the most exhausting sort.*

BARBARA GRIZZUTI HARRISON

Every good thought you think is contributing its share to the ultimate result of your life.

GRENVILLE KLEISER

Don't be afraid your life will end; be afraid that it will never begin.

— GRACE HANSEN

I have learned this at least by my experiment: that if one advances confidently in the direction of his dreams, and endeavors to live the life which he has imagined, he will meet with a success unexpected in common hours.

Henry David Thoreau

We have to learn to be our own best friends because we fall too easily into the trap of being our worst enemies.

Roderick Thorp

It is never too late to be what you might have been.

GEORGE ELIOT

*H*ere's one thing I've said many times to the people I've encouraged along and I hope you will remember it. If you *want* to make it, you can. You *can* move up the level system. You *can* become confident in yourself. You *can* graduate, if you *want* to.

Annabel Victoria Safire

*The important thing is
to learn a lesson
every time you lose.*

— JOHN McENROE

Happiness in the older years of life, like happiness in every year of life, is a matter of choice——your choice for yourself.

HAROLD AZINE

Never bend your head. Always hold it high. Look the world straight in the eye.

HELEN KELLER

The hopeful man sees success where others see failure, sunshine where others see shadows and storm.

O. S. MARDEN

Write it in your heart that every day is the best day in the year.

RALPH WALDO EMERSON

It is a common experience that a problem difficult at night is resolved in the morning after the committee of sleep has worked on it.

JOHN STEINBECK

> Be not afraid of life.
> Believe that life is worth
> living, and your belief will
> help create the fact.

HENRY JAMES

For a man to achieve all that is demanded of him he must regard himself as greater than he is.

JOHANN WOLFGANG VON GOETHE

He that is of a merry heart hath a continual feast.

PROVERBS 15:15

*Be a friend to yourself,
and others will.*

SCOTTISH PROVERB

*Y*our success and happiness lie in you.
External conditions are the accidents of life.
The great enduring realities are love and
service. Joy is the holy fire that keeps our
purpose warm and our intelligence aglow.
Resolve to keep happy, and your joy and you
shall form an invincible host against difficulty.

Helen Keller

*I celebrate myself,
and sing myself.*

WALT WHITMAN

To be nobody but yourself—in a world which is doing its best, night and day, to make you everybody else—means to fight the hardest battle which any human being can fight, and never stop fighting.

e.e. cummings

Nothing can bring you peace but yourself.

RALPH WALDO EMERSON

If you have no confidence in self you are twice defeated in the race of life. With confidence, you have won even before you have started.

Marcus Garvey

Unrest of spirit is a mark of life;
one problem after another presents itself
and in the solving of them we can find
our greatest pleasure.

Karl Menninger

We must accept finite disappointment, but we must never lose infinite hope.

— Martin Luther King, Jr.

For myself I am an optimist——it does not seem to be much use being anything else.

WINSTON CHURCHILL

Neglect not the gift that is in thee.

I TIMOTHY 4:14

He has called on the best that was in us. There was no such thing as half-trying. Whether it was running a race or catching a football, competing in school—we were to try. And we were to try harder than anyone else. We might not be the best, and none of us were, but we were to make the effort to be the best. "After you have done the best you can," he used to say, "the hell with it."

*Senator Robert F. Kennedy,
tribute to his father, Joseph P. Kennedy*

No one can make you feel inferior without your consent.

ELEANOR ROOSEVELT

I don't believe in pessimism. If something doesn't come up the way you want, forge ahead. If you think it's going to rain, it will.

— *Clint Eastwood* —

Waste no more time arguing what a good man should be. Be one.

MARCUS AURELIUS

If you think you'll lose, you're lost,
For out in the world we find
Success begins with a fellow's will;
It's all in the state of mind.

Life's battles don't always go
To the stronger or faster man;
But soon or late the man who wins
Is the man who thinks he can.

Walter D. Wintle

Everything that enlarges the sphere of human powers, that shows man he can do what he thought he could not do, is valuable.

— *Samuel Johnson*

Believe that you have it,
and you have it.

(Credo quod habes, et habes.)

Desiderius Erasmus

I firmly believe that if you follow a path that interests you, not to the exclusion of love, sensitivity, and cooperation with others, but with the strength of conviction that you can move others by your own efforts, and do not make success or failure the criteria by which you live, the chances are you'll be a person worthy of your own respect.

Neil Simon

I am an idealist. I don't know where I am going but I'm on my way.

CARL SANDBURG

Hope is the pillar that holds up the world. Hope is the dream of a waking man.

— PLINY THE ELDER

Hope is wanting something so eagerly that—in spite of all the evidence that you're not going to get it—you go right on wanting it. And the remarkable thing about it is that this very act of hoping produces a kind of strength of its own.

Norman Vincent Peale

If you're feeling good about you, what you're wearing outside doesn't mean a thing.

LEONTYNE PRICE

As I grow to understand life less and less, I learn to live it more and more.

JULES RENARD

Long-term change requires looking honestly at our lives and realizing that it's nice to be needed, but not at the expense of our health, our happiness, and our sanity.

— *Ellen Sue Stern* —

I have an everyday religion that works for me. Love yourself first and everything else falls into line. You really have to love yourself to get anything done in this world.

Lucille Ball

Today a new sun rises for me; everything lives, everything is animated, everything seems to speak to me of my passion, everything invites me to cherish it . . .

— *Anne de Lenclos*

Trust thyself: every heart vibrates to that iron string.

RALPH WALDO EMERSON

You never really lose until you quit trying.

— MIKE DITKA

I would have you a man of sense as well as sensibility. You will find goodness and truth everywhere you go. If you have to choose, choose truth. For that is closest to Earth. Keep close to Earth, my boy: in that lies strength. Simplicity of heart is just as necessary to an architect as for a farmer or a minister if the architect is going to build great buildings.

*Ann Wright,
to her son Frank Lloyd Wright*

The best way to secure future happiness is to be as happy as is rightfully possible today.

CHARLES W. ELIOT

To fill the hour—that is happiness; to fill the hour, and leave no crevice for a repentance or an approval.

RALPH WALDO EMERSON

Happiness consists not in having much, but in being content with little.

Marguerite
Countess of Blessington

... Whatever your labors and aspirations, in the noisy confusion of life, keep peace in your soul. With all its sham, drudgery, and broken dreams, it is still a beautiful world. Be cheerful. Strive to be happy.

Max Ehrmann

Whate'er your lot may be,

Paddle your own canoe.

EDWARD P. PHILPOTS

Happy is the soul that has something to look backward to with pride, and something to look forward to with hope.

OLIVER G. WILSON

Integrate what you believe into every single area of your life. Take your heart to work and ask the most and best of everybody else. Don't let your special character and values, the secret that you know and no one else does, the truth—don't let that get swallowed up by the great chewing complacency.

Meryl Streep

Love your friend and look to yourself.

SCOTTISH PROVERB

The greatest possession is self-possession.

ETHEL WATTS MUMFORD

Know then,
whatever cheerful and serene
Supports the mind, supports the body too:
Hence, the most vital movement mortals feel
Is hope, the balm and lifeblood of the soul.

John Armstrong

It is impossible to live a pleasant life
without living wisely, well, and justly,
and it is impossible to live wisely,
well, and justly without living pleasantly.

Epicurus

*K*eep love in your heart. A life without it is like a sunless garden when the flowers are dead. The consciousness of loving and being loved brings a warmth and richness to life that nothing else can bring.

Oscar Wilde

I can live for two months on a good compliment.

MARK TWAIN

*Laugh at yourself first,
before anyone else can.*

ELSA MAXWELL

Never mention the worst. Never think of it. Drop it out of your consciousness. At least ten times every day affirm, "I expect the best and with God's help will attain the best." In so doing your thoughts will turn toward the best and become conditioned to its realization.

Norman Vincent Peale

Be yourself. Who else is better qualified?

— Frank J. Giblin II

*If you do not hope,
you will not find
what is beyond your hopes.*

~~~

St. Clement of Alexandria

Learn what you are, and be such.

PINDAR

Every life is its own excuse for being, and to deny or refute the untrue things that are said of you is an error in judgment. All wrong recoils upon the doer, and the man who makes wrong statements about others is himself to be pitied, not the man he vilifies. It is better to be lied about than to lie. At the last no one can harm us but ourselves.

Elbert Hubbard

Become a possibilitarian. No matter how dark things seem to be or actually are, raise your sights and see the possibilities—always see them, for they're always there.

Norman Vincent Peale

Live all you can; it's a mistake not to. It doesn't so much matter what you do in particular so long as you have your life.

— *Henry James*

To be able to look back upon one's past life with satisfaction is to live twice.

MARTIAL

Believe in life! Always human beings will live and progress to greater, broader, and fuller life.

W. E. B. Du Bois

If you think you can, you can. And if you think you can't, you're right.

MARY KAY ASH

*L*ife is a series of surprises. We do not guess today the mood, the pleasure, the power of tomorrow, when we are building up our being.

Ralph Waldo Emerson

You don't just stumble into the future. You create your own future.

ROGER SMITH

One of the things I learned the hard way was that it doesn't pay to get discouraged. Keeping busy and making optimism a way of life can restore your faith in yourself.

Lucille Ball

If you practice an art, be proud of it and make it proud of you.... It may break your heart, but it will fill your heart before it breaks it: it will make you a person in your own right.

— *Maxwell Anderson*

When we cannot find contentment in ourselves, it is useless to seek it elsewhere.

— La Rochefoucauld

The greatest mistake you can make in life is to be continually fearing you will make one.

ELBERT HUBBARD

Always give your best, never get discouraged, never be petty; always remember, others may hate you. Those who hate you don't win unless you hate them. And then you destroy yourself.

Richard M. Nixon

Great thoughts always come from the heart.

MARQUIS DE VAUVENARGUES

*H*old your head high, stick your chest out. You can make it. It gets dark sometimes but morning comes. . . . Keep hope alive.

Reverend Jesse Jackson

It takes seventeen muscles to smile and forty-three to frown.

SAYING

Do not seek to have everything that happens happen as you wish, but wish for everything to happen as it actually does happen, and your life will be serene.

Epictetus

I also know that when I'm trusting and being myself as fully as possible, everything in my life reflects this by falling into place easily, often miraculously.

Shakti Gawain

If it were not for hopes,
the heart would break.

THOMAS FULLER

As soon as you trust yourself, you will know how to live.

— Johann Wolfgang von Goethe

And, above all things, never think that you're not good enough yourself. A man should never think that. My belief is that in life people will take you very much at your own reckoning.

Anthony Trollope

Every man is the architect of his own fortune.

— ENGLISH PROVERB

When one door shuts another opens. He that would struggle with the world, and bear up in adversity, ought still to resolve not to be discouraged, for resolution is the mother of fortitude, and not only necessary to our support, but very much conducive to our deliverance.

Samuel Palmer

Everything comes to him who hustles while he waits.

THOMAS ALVA EDISON

Fear less, hope more; eat less, chew more; whine less, breathe more; talk less, say more; hate less, love more; and all good things are yours.

Anonymous

I am as bad as the worst, but, thank God, I am as good as the best.

WALT WHITMAN

> *Resolve to be thyself:*
> *and know that he*
> *Who finds himself,*
> *loses his misery.*

— MATTHEW ARNOLD

*Trust your hopes,
not your fears.*

DAVID MAHONEY

Knowledge of what is possible is the beginning of happiness.

GEORGE SANTAYANA

Look, I really don't want to wax philosophic, but I will say that if you're alive, you got to flap your arms and legs, you got to jump around a lot, you got to make a lot of noise, because life is the very opposite of death. And, therefore, as I see it, if you're quiet, you're not living . . . you've got to be noisy, or at least your *thoughts* should be noisy and colorful and lively.

Mel Brooks

Laffing iz the sensation ov pheeling good all over, and showing it principally in one spot.

H. W. SHAW

Endure, and preserve yourselves for better things.

V̄IRGIL

He who has confidence in himself will lead the rest.

HORACE

If we spend our lives in loving, we have no leisure to complain, or to feel unhappiness.

JOSEPH JOUBERT

To be a great champion you must believe you are the best. If you're not, pretend you are.

MUHAMMAD ALI

*O*ne of the best safeguards of our hopes, I have suggested, is to be able to mark off the areas of hopelessness and to acknowledge them, to face them directly, not with despair but with the creative intent of keeping them from polluting all the areas of possibility.

William F. Lynch

Be content with such things as ye have.

HEBREWS 13:5

I am as my Creator made me, and since He is satisfied, so am I.

MINNIE SMITH

You need to claim the events of your life to make yourself yours. When you truly possess all you have been and done, which may take some time, you are fierce with reality.

— Florida Scott Maxwell

The man who makes no mistakes does not usually make anything.

EDWARD JOHN PHELPS

Happiness depends upon ourselves.

— ARISTOTLE

Maintain a sense of perspective and proportion in all your endeavors. . . . Don't let problems and setbacks block out the light of reason. The human mind is like a magnifying glass: It exaggerates. A simple rule of thumb: Whatever you're looking at is not as big a deal as you think it is.

Daniel Meacham

> Man who man would be,
> must rule the empire
> of himself.

— PERCY BYSSHE SHELLY

One needs something to believe in, something for which one can have whole-hearted enthusiasm. One needs to feel that one's life has meaning, that one is needed in this world.

Hannah Senesh

While one person hesitates because he feels inferior, the other is busy making mistakes and becoming superior.

— Henry C. Link

Trust thyself only, and another shall not betray thee.

Thomas Fuller

I think these difficult times have helped me to understand better than before how infinitely rich and beautiful life is in every way and that so many things that one goes around worrying about are of no importance whatsoever.

— *Isak Dinesen*

If you can't go over, you must go under.

— JEWISH PROVERB

Don't try to be such a perfect girl, darling. Do the best you can without too much anxiety or strain.

— JESSE BARNARD

There is nothing like a dream to create the future.

VICTOR HUGO

Work out your own salvation.

PHILIPPIANS 2:12

Learn to get in touch with silence within yourself and know that everything in this life has a purpose. There are no mistakes, no coincidences, all events are blessings given to us to learn from.

— Elizabeth Kübler-Ross

Keep making the movements of life.

THORNTON WILDER

She didn't know it couldn't be done so she went ahead and did it.

MARY'S ALMANAC

It is only because of problems that we grow mentally and spiritually.

M. Scott Peck

Live every day as if it were your last. Do every job as if you were the boss. Drive as if all other vehicles were police cars. Treat everybody else as if he were you.

— Phoenix Flame —

We know too much and feel too little. At least we feel too little of those creative emotions from which a good life springs.

— *Bertrand Russell* —

It is not how much we have, but how much we enjoy, that makes happiness.

CHARLES HADDON SPURGEON

When you come to the end of your rope, tie a knot and hang on.

ATTRIBUTED TO
FRANKLIN D. ROOSEVELT

When the going gets tough, the tough get going.

SAYING

Joy is what happens to us when we allow ourselves to recognize how good things really are.

MARIANNE WILLIAMSON

The supreme happiness of life is the conviction that we are loved.

VICTOR HUGO

If you really do put a small value upon yourself, rest assured that the world will not raise your price.

A<small>NONYMOUS</small>

Within us we have a hope which always walks in front of our present narrow experience; it is the undying faith in the infinite in us.

Rabindranath Tagore

Be glad today.
Tomorrow may bring tears.
Be brave today. The darkest night will pass.
And golden rays will usher in the dawn.
Who conquers now shall rule the coming years.

Sarah Knowles Bolton

*If I can make it,
you can make it.*

REVEREND JESSE JACKSON

The turning point in the process of growing up is when you discover the core of strength within you that survives all hurt.

Max Lerner

Anything you're good at contributes to happiness.

BERTRAND RUSSELL

Always look out for the sunlight the Lord sends into your days.

HOPE CAMPBELL

Courage is doing what you are afraid to do. There can be no courage unless you're scared.

EDDIE RICKENBACKER

*Do what you can,
with what you have,
where you are.*

THEODORE ROOSEVELT

He who has health has hope. And he who has hope has everything.

— ARABIAN PROVERB

In doing good, avoid fame. In doing bad, avoid disgrace. Pursue a middle course as your principle. Thus you will guard your body from harm, preserve your life, fulfill your duties by your parents, and live your alloted span of life.

Chuangtse

*Be cheerful
while you are alive.*

— PTAHHOTPE

It is only with the heart that one can see rightly; what is essential is invisible to the eye.

SAINT-EXUPÉRY

*Make a crutch
of your cross.*

ENGLISH PROVERB

The good life, as I conceive it, is a happy life. I do not mean that if you are good you will be happy; I mean that if you are happy you will be good.

Bertrand Russell

Hope ever tells us tomorrow will be better.

TIBULLUS

The more I want to get something done, the less I call it work.

RICHARD BACH

Do not take life too seriously. You will never get out of it alive.

ELBERT HUBBARD

It is better to be happy

for a moment

and be burned up with beauty

than to live a long time

and be bored all the while.

— *Don Marquis* —

There is only one way to happiness and that is to cease worrying about things which are beyond the power of our will.

Epictetus

Hope, child, tomorrow and tomorrow still,
And every tomorrow hope; trust while you live.
Hope, each time the dawn doth heaven fill,
Be there to ask as God is there to give.

Victor Hugo

It is as healthy to enjoy sentiment as to enjoy jam.

G. K. CHESTERTON

The trick is not how much pain you feel—but how much joy you feel. Any idiot can feel pain. Life is full of excuses to feel pain, excuses not to live, excuses, excuses, excuses.

— *Erica Jong* —

The greatest wealth is
to live content with little,
for there is never want
where the mind is satisfied.

LUCRETIUS

Respect yourself if you would have others respect you.

BALTASAR GRACIÁN

> *F*ind expression for a sorrow,
> and it will become dear to you.
> Find expression for a joy, and
> you will intensify its ecstasy.

Oscar Wilde

Whatever comes, let's be content withall:
Among God's blessings there is no one small.

— *Robert Herrick*

*Happiness is a habit—
cultivate it.*

ELBERT HUBBARD

You don't get to choose how you're going to die. Or when. You can only decide how you're going to live. Now.

— Joan Baez —

I like living. I have sometimes been wildly, despairingly, acutely miserable, racked with sorrow, but through it all I still know quite certainly that just to *be alive* is a grand thing.

Agatha Christie

You win some, you lose some, and some get rained out, but you gotta suit up for them all.

J. ASKENBERG

You have to believe in happiness or happiness never comes.

— Douglas Malloch

The one important thing I have learned over the years is the difference between taking one's work seriously and taking one's self seriously. The first is imperative and the second is disastrous.

Will Durant

Above all, challenge yourself. You may well surprise yourself at what strengths you have, what you can accomplish.

Cecile M. Springer

He who cannot rest, cannot work;

he who cannot let go, cannot hold on;

he who cannot find footing,

cannot go forward.

Harry Emerson Fosdick

Confront the dark parts of yourself, and work to banish them with illumination and forgiveness. Your willingness to wrestle with your demons will cause your angels to sing. Use the pain as fuel, as a reminder of your strength.

August Wilson

It's such an act of optimism to get through a day and enjoy it and laugh and do all that without thinking about death. What spirit human beings have!

— *Gilda Radner* —

Don't wish me happiness—I don't expect to be happy . . . it's gotten beyond that somehow. Wish me courage and strength and a sense of humor—I will need them all.

Anne Morrow Lindbergh

Some men go through life absolutely miserable because, despite the most enormous achievement, they just didn't do one thing—like the architect who didn't build St. Paul's. I didn't quite build St. Paul's, but I stood on more mountaintops than possibly I deserved.

Lord Thorneycroft (Peter Thorneycroft)

To hope is to enjoy.

JACQUES DELILLE

The first and great commandment is, Don't let them scare you.

ELMER DAVIS

*L*ife can be wildly tragic at times, and I've had my share. But whatever happens to you, you have to keep a slightly comic attitude. In the final analysis, you have got not to forget to laugh.

Katharine Hepburn

If at first you don't succeed, try, try again.

SAYING

Never let the fear of striking out get in your way.

George Herman
"Babe" Ruth

[Today's students] can put dope in their veins or hope in their brains. . . . If they can conceive it and believe it, they can achieve it. They must know it is not their aptitude but their attitude that will determine their altitude.

Reverend Jesse Jackson

Self-help must precede help from others. Even for making certain of help from heaven, one has to help oneself.

Morarji R. Desai

First ask yourself: What is the worst that can happen? Then prepare to accept it. Then proceed to improve on the worst.

— Dale Carnegie

Life is worth living . . . since it is what we make it . . .

— WILLIAM JAMES

Where your pleasure is, there is your treasure; where your treasure, there your heart; where your heart, there your happiness.

— *St. Augustine*

Like an ox-cart driver in monsoon season or the skipper of a grounded ship, one must sometimes go forward by going back.

John Barth

Compassion for myself is the most powerful healer of them all.

THEODORE ISAAC RUBIN

May we never let the things we can't have, or don't have, or shouldn't have, spoil our enjoyment of the things we do have and can have. As we value our happiness let us not forget it, for one of the greatest lessons in life is learning to be happy without the things we cannot or should not have.

Richard L. Evans

The brave man is not
he who feels no fear,
For that were stupid and irrational;
But he, whose noble soul its fears subdues,
And bravely dares the danger
nature shrinks from.

Joanna Baillie

Hope to the end.

1 PETER 1:13

If I were asked to give what I consider the single most useful bit of advice for all humanity, it would be this: Expect trouble as an inevitable part of life, and when it comes, hold your head high, look it squarely in the eye and say, "I will be bigger than you. You cannot defeat me."
Then repeat to yourself the most comforting of all words,
"This too shall pass."
Maintaining self-respect in the face of a devastating experience is of prime importance.

Ann Landers

The secret of how to live without resentment or embarrassment in a world in which I was different from everyone else . . . was to be indifferent to that difference.

— *Al Capp* —

Joy is the echo of God's life within us.

JOSEPH MARMION

The inner side of every cloud
Is bright and shining;
Therefore I turn my clouds about,
And always wear them inside out,
To show the lining.

❦

Ellen Thornycroft Fowler Felkin

I live, which is the main point.

HEINRICH HEINE

You're gonna have your ups and downs and your moments when you call it quits. You gotta stick it out, because there's only one ballgame here, and it's your own life. You got no choice. You got to play to win if you want to stay on this earth.

advice given to cancer patient James Brown by another patient

> *No man knows what he can do till he tries.*

— PUBLILIUS SYRUS

Take plenty of time to count your blessings, but never spend a minute in worry.

— Anonymous

Don't be sad, don't be angry, if life deceives you! Submit to your grief—your time for joy will come, believe me.

Aleksandr Sergeyevich Pushkin

Do continue to believe that with your feeling and your work you are taking part in the greatest; the more strongly you cultivate in yourself this belief, the more will reality and the world go forth from it.

Rainer Maria Rilke

Be happy. It is a way of being wise.

COLETTE

When I look in the glass I see that every line in my face means pessimism, but in spite of my face—that is my experience—I remain an optimist.

— Richard Jefferies

Do not craze yourself
with thinking, but go about
your business anywhere. Life is not
intellectual and critical, but sturdy.

Ralph Waldo Emerson

... Your ability to go through life successfully will depend largely upon your travelling with courage and a good sense of humor, for both are conditions of survival. . . .

John R. Silber

There is a real magic in enthusiasm. It spells the difference between mediocrity and accomplishment. . . . It gives warmth and good feeling to all your personal relationships.

Norman Vincent Peale

Anyone's a fool who doesn't try to live up to his dreams and abilities.

SAYING

Joy makes us giddy.

— G. E. Lessing

Part II

The Positive Perspective

No matter how far you have gone on a wrong road, turn back.

TURKISH PROVERB

This is the best day the world has ever seen. Tomorrow will be better.

R. A. CAMPBELL

Little deeds of kindness,
little words of love,
Help to make earth happy
like the heaven above.

JULIA A. FLETCHER CARNEY

The world is round and the place which may seem like the end may also be the beginning.

IVY BAKER PRIEST

Earth's crammed with heaven.

ELIZABETH BARRETT BROWNING

The year's at the spring
And day's at the morn;
Morning's at seven;
The hillside's dew-pearled;
The lark's on the wing;
The snail's on the thorn:
God's in his heaven—
All's right with the world.

Robert Browning

Those who bring sunshine to the lives of others cannot keep it from themselves.

JAMES M. BARRIE

Gray skies are just clouds passing over.

— DUKE ELLINGTON

Never stop. One always stops as soon as something is about to happen.

PETER BROOK

When faced with a
decision, I always ask,
"What would be
the most fun?"

PEGGY WALKER

Anyone can carry his burden, however hard, until nightfall. Anyone can do his work, however hard, for one day. Anyone can live sweetly, patiently, lovingly, purely, till the sun goes down. And this is all that life really means.

attributed to Robert Louis Stevenson by Senator Sam Erwin

The most beautiful thing in the world is, of course, the world itself.

WALLACE STEVENS

One must act in painting as in life, directly.

PABLO PICASSO

*O*pen your eyes! The world is still intact; it is as pristine as it was on the first day, as fresh as milk!

PAUL CLAUDEL

Life is a short affair;
We should try to make it
smooth, and free from strife.

— EURIPIDES

*I've never seen
a monument erected to
a pessimist.*

~~~

PAUL HARVEY

Stand up straight. Admire the world. Relish the love of a gentle woman. Trust in the Lord.

JOHN CHEEVER

In this best of all possible worlds . . . all is for the best.

VOLTAIRE

Love makes people look at the bright side of things. They do see the bad things, but they make a great effort to see the good, so they do see the good.

Anonymous

'Tis always morning somewhere.

HENRY WADSWORTH LONGFELLOW

No pessimist ever discovered the secrets of the stars, or sailed to an uncharted land, or opened a new heaven to the human spirit.

Helen Keller

> When things go wrong—
> don't go with them.
>
> — ANONYMOUS

But friendship is precious, not only in the shade, but in the sunshine of life; and thanks to a benevolent arrangement of things, the greater part of life is sunshine.

President Thomas Jefferson

*The world is so full of
a number of things,
I'm sure we should all be
as happy as kings.*

ROBERT LOUIS STEVENSON

Make a rule, and pray to God to help you to keep it, never, if possible, to lie down at night without being able to say: "I have made one human being at least a little wiser, or a little happier, or at least a little better this day."

— *Charles Kingsley* —

Flowers grow out of dark moments.

— CORITA KENT

Trust men, and they will be true to you; treat them greatly, and they will show themselves great.

RALPH WALDO EMERSON

Life is a great big canvas; throw all the paint on it you can.

— Danny Kaye

*A baby is God's opinion
that life should go on.*

— CARL SANDBURG

It is the formidable character of the species to routinely seek the improbable, the difficult, even the impossible, as a source of pleasure and self-justification. Who would try to write poems, or novels, or paint pictures unless he is an optimist?

Lionel Tiger

Laughter makes good blood.

— ITALIAN PROVERB

How good is man's life, the mere living! how fit to employ All the heart and the soul and the sense forever in joy!

ROBERT BROWNING

While there's life there's hope.

English proverb, borrowed from Cicero

Let me win, but if I cannot win, let me be brave in the attempt.

SPECIAL OLYMPICS MOTTO

We are all here for a spell; get all the good laughs you can.

WILL ROGERS

*Caring about others,
running the risk of feeling,
and leaving an impact on
people bring happiness.*

RABBI HAROLD KUSHNER

Always do right. This will gratify some people and astonish the rest.

MARK TWAIN

The great pleasure in life is doing what people say you cannot do.

— WALTER BAGEHOT

Be civil to all; sociable to many; familiar with few; Friend to one; Enemy to none.

— Benjamin Franklin

Ideals are like stars; you will not succeed in touching them with your hands, but like the seafaring man . . . you choose them as your guides, and following them you will reach your destiny.

— Carl Schurz

*Life's a pleasant institution;
Let us take it as it comes.*

W. S. GILBERT

*To be happy and contented,
count your blessings,
not your cash.*

CHINESE PROVERB

Everything that is done in the world is done by hope.

MARTIN LUTHER

It has never been, and never will be, easy work! But the road that is built in hope is more pleasant to the traveler than the road built in despair, even though they both lead to the same destination.

Marion Zimmer Bradley

The best portion of
a good man's life,
His little, nameless, unremembered acts
Of kindness and of love.

William Wordsworth

I don't say embrace trouble. That's as bad as treating it as an enemy. But I do say meet it as a friend, for you'll see a lot of it and had better be on speaking terms with it.

— Oliver Wendell Holmes, Jr.

Life is short; live it up.

— NIKITA KHRUSHCHEV

It is better to live one day as a lion than a hundred years as a sheep.
(*Meglio vivere un giorno da leone che cento anni da pecora.*)

motto on Italian twenty-lire silver piece, c. 1930

Everything is miraculous. It is miraculous that one does not melt in one's bath.

PICASSO, ATTRIBUTED

*Love is all we have,
the only way that each
can help the other.*

EURIPIDES

If we had no winter, the spring would not be so pleasant: if we did not sometimes taste of adversity, prosperity would not be so welcome.

Anne Bradstreet

*The most wasted day
of all is that on which
we have not laughed.*

SÉBASTIEN CHAMFORT

Life is still beautiful.

~

J. C. F. SCHILLER

Although the world is full of suffering, it is full also of the overcoming of it.

— HELEN KELLER

Always do what you are afraid to do.

ANONYMOUS

Few will have the greatness to bend history itself; but each of us can work to change a small portion of events, and in the total of all those acts will be written the history of this generation.

Senator Robert F. Kennedy

Some of the most rewarding and beautiful moments of a friendship happen in the unforeseen open spaces between planned activities. It is important that you allow these spaces to exist.

Christine Leefeldt and Ernest Callenbach

I long to accomplish a great and noble task, but it is my chief duty to accomplish small tasks as if they were great and noble.

Helen Keller

Walk on a rainbow trail;
walk on a trail of song,
and all about you will be beauty.
There is a way out of every dark mist,
over a rainbow trail.

Navajo song

We find a delight in the beauty and happiness of children, that makes the heart too big for the body.

RALPH WALDO EMERSON

Without belittling the courage with which men have died, we should not forget those acts of courage with which men . . . have *lived*. The courage of life is often a less dramatic spectacle than the courage of a final moment; but it is no less a magnificent mixture of triumph and tragedy. A man does what he must—in spite of personal consequences, in spite of obstacles and dangers and pressures—and that is the basis of all human morality . . .

Senator John F. Kennedy

After all, tomorrow is another day.

— MARGARET MITCHELL

> When you reach for the stars, you may not quite get them, but you won't come up with a handful of mud either.
>
> LEO BURNETT

Don't hurry, don't worry. You're only here for a short visit. So be sure to stop and smell the flowers.

WALTER HAGEN

> The way I see it, if you want the rainbow, you gotta put up with the rain.
>
> — DOLLY PARTON

Love the moment, and the energy of that moment will spread beyond all boundaries.

CORITA KENT

Hopeful as the break of day.

THOMAS BAILEY ALDRICH

Far away there in the sunshine are my highest aspirations. I may not reach them but I can look up and see their beauty, believe in them, and try to follow them.

— Louisa May Alcott

The human heart refuses to believe in a universe without a purpose.

—Immanuel Kant

Light tomorrow with today.

— ELIZABETH BARRETT BROWNING

> To me every hour of the light and dark is a miracle,
> Every cubic inch of space is a miracle.

WALT WHITMAN

Make it a rule of life never to regret and never look back. Regret is an appalling waste of energy; you can't build on it; it is good only for wallowing in.

Katherine Mansfield

Life is sweet.

ENGLISH PROVERB

Never give up on anybody.

HUBERT H. HUMPHREY

For me, a hearty "belly laugh" is one of the beautiful sounds in the world.

BENNETT CERF

It matters not how long you live, but how well.

PUBLILIUS SYRUS

Don't evaluate your life in terms of achievements, trivial *or* monumental, along the way. . . . Instead, wake up and appreciate everything you encounter along your path. Enjoy the flowers that are there for your pleasure. Tune in to the sunrise, the little children, the laughter, the rain, and the birds. Drink it all in . . . there is no way to happiness; happiness *is* the way.

Dr. Wayne W. Dyer

I will turn their mourning into joy, and will comfort them, and make them rejoice from their sorrow.

JEREMIAH 31:13

If you shut your door to all errors, truth will be shut out.

RABINDRANATH TAGORE

Optimism doesn't wait on facts. It deals with prospects. Pessimism is a waste of time.

— Norman Cousins

Some people are always grumbling because roses have thorns; I am thankful that thorns have roses.

ALPHONSE KARR

Nor love thy life, nor hate;
but what thou liv'st.
Live well; how long or short
permit to Heaven.

JOHN MILTON

I have found that there is a tremendous joy in giving. It is a very important part of the joy of living.

WILLIAM BLACK

*All life is an experiment.
The more experiments you
make the better.*

~

RALPH WALDO EMERSON

If you are wise, laugh.

MARTIAL

Our lives are like the course of the sun. At the darkest moment there is the promise of daylight.

LONDON TIMES

Life is real! Life is earnest!
And the grave is not its goal.

H‍ENRY W‍ADSWORTH
L‍ONGFELLOW

Make yourself necessary to somebody.

~

RALPH WALDO EMERSON

Often the test of courage is not to die but to live.

— Vittorio Alfieri

It just ain't possible to explain some things. It's interesting to wonder on them and do some speculation, but the main thing is you have to accept it—take it for what it is, and get on with your growing.

— *Jim Dodge*

What time is it?
Time to do well,

Time to live better,

Give up that grudge,

Answer that letter,

Speak the kind word to sweeten a sorrow,

Do that kind deed you would leave 'till tomorrow.

Anonymous

Something will turn up.

BENJAMIN DISRAELI

Use no hurtful deceit; think innocently and justly and, if you speak, speak accordingly.

BENJAMIN FRANKLIN

We should never despair, our situation before has been unpromising and has changed for the better, so I trust, it will again. If new difficulties arise, we must only put forth new exertions and proportion our efforts to the exigency of the times.

General George Washington

The follies which a man regrets most in his life are those which he didn't commit when he had the opportunity.

— Helen Rowland

Pick battles big enough to matter, small enough to win.

— JONATHAN KOZOL

Take short views, hope for the best, and trust in God.

SYDNEY SMITH

Derive happiness in oneself from a good day's work, from illuminating the fog that surrounds us.

HENRI MATISSE

Life was meant to be lived, and curiosity must be kept alive. One must never, for whatever reason, turn his back on life.

— *Eleanor Roosevelt*

The gloom of the world is but a shadow.
Behind it, yet within our reach, is joy. There is
radiance and glory in the darkness, could we but
see; and to see, we have only to look.
Life is so generous a giver, but we, judging its gifts by
their covering, cast them away as ugly or heavy or hard.
Remove the covering, and you will find beneath it a
living splendour, woven of love, by wisdom, with power.

Fra Giovanni

Associate yourself with men of good quality if you esteem your own reputation; for 'tis better to be alone than in bad company.

George Washington

May the road rise to meet you.
May the wind be ever at your back.
May the Good Lord keep you in the hollow of His hand.
May your heart be as warm as your hearthstone.
And when you come to die
may the wail of the poor
be the only sorrow
you'll leave behind.
May God bless you always.

Anonymous

Discover day-to-day excitement.

CHARLES BAUDELAIRE

> The most I can do for my friend is simply to be his friend.

— Henry David Thoreau

To look up and not down,
To look forward and not back,
To look out and not in, and
To lend a hand.

Edward Everett Hale

Einstein's three rules of work:

(1) Out of clutter find simplicity.

(2) From discord make harmony.

(3) In the middle of difficulty lies opportunity.

Albert Einstein

I am not a perfect servant. I am a public servant doing my best against the odds. As I develop and serve, be patient. God is not finished with me yet.

Reverend Jesse Jackson

Don't do things to not die, do things to enjoy living. The by-product may be not dying.

Bernie S. Siegel, M.D.

Be not too critical of others, and love much.

— JULIA HUXLEY

> *All of us do not have equal talent, but all of us should have an equal opportunity to develop our talent.*
>
> — JOHN F. KENNEDY

Weeping may endure for a night, but joy cometh in the morning.

PSALMS 30:5

*L*eave tomorrow's trouble to tomorrow's strength; tomorrow's work to tomorrow's time; tomorrow's trial to tomorrow's grace and to tomorrow's God.

Anonymous

*Do not bind yourself to
what you cannot do.*

GEORGE SHELLEY

I take a simple view of living. It is keep your eyes open and get on with it.

LAURENCE OLIVIER

Keep company with those who may make you better.

ENGLISH SAYING

Life is good only when it is magical and musical, a perfect timing and consent, and when we do not anatomize it. You must treat the days respectfully, you must be a day yourself, and not interrogate it like a college professor. The world is enigmatical,—everything said, and everything known or done—and must not be taken literally, but genially.

Ralph Waldo Emerson

My advice to you is not to inquire why or whither, but just enjoy your ice cream while it's on your plate—that's my philosophy.

— Thornton Wilder —

Instead of loving your enemy, treat your friend a little better.

EDGAR WATSON HOWE

Never look back unless you are planning to go that way.

— SAYING

The happiest business in all the world is
that of making friends,
And no investment on the street pays larger dividends,
For life is more than stocks and bonds,
and love than rate percent,
And he who gives in friendship's name shall reap
what he has spent.

Anne S. Eaton

Wish not so much to live long as to live well.

— Benjamin Franklin

Mighty oaks from little acorns grow.

SAYING

No person who is enthusiastic about his work has anything to fear from life.

SAMUEL GOLDWYN

*Goodness is uneventful.
It does not flash, it glows.*

DAVID GRAYSON

But the nearer the dawn the darker the night,
And by going wrong all things come right;
Things have been mended that were worse,
And the worse, the nearer they are to mend.

Henry Wadsworth Longfellow

I have a simple philosophy. Fill what's empty. Empty what's full. And scratch where it itches.

— ALICE ROOSEVELT LONGWORTH

The only way of finding the limits of the possible is by going beyond them into the impossible.

ARTHUR C. CLARKE

Live not as though there were a thousand years ahead of you. Fate is at your elbow; make yourself good while life and power are still yours.

— *Marcus Aurelius*

Nothing is too small to know, and nothing too big to attempt.

WILLIAM VAN HORNE

> *In spite of all our hopes, dreams, and efforts, change is real and forever. Accept it fearlessly. Investigate the unknown; neither fear nor worship it.*
>
> — Joseph A. Bauer

When you have only two pennies left in the world, buy a loaf of bread with one, and a lily with the other.

CHINESE PROVERB

Is life worth living? It is, so you take the risk of getting up in the morning and going through the day's work.

WALTER PERSEGATI

*H*appiness is like a cat. If you try to coax it or call it, it will avoid you. It will never come. But if you pay no attention to it and go about your business, you'll find it rubbing against your legs and jumping into your lap. So forget pursuing happiness. Pin your hopes on work, on family, on learning, on knowing, on loving. Forget pursuing happiness, pursue these other things, and with luck happiness will come.

William Bennett

*If you want to be loved,
love and be lovable.*

BENJAMIN FRANKLIN

> When nothing is sure,
> everything is possible.
>
> — Margaret Drabble

Once you have been confronted with a life-and-death situation, trivia no longer matters. Your perspective grows and you live at a deeper level. There's no time for pettiness.

Margaretta "Happy" Rockefeller

Let us not bankrupt our todays by paying interest on the regrets of yesterday and by borrowing in advance the troubles of tomorrow.

Ralph W. Sockman

*Don't fix the blame,
fix the problem.*

— KEITH S. PENNINGTON

Life just is. You have to flow with it. Give yourself to the moment. Let it happen.

GOVERNOR JERRY BROWN

*The mere sense of living
is joy enough.*

EMILY DICKINSON

> *One of the things I keep learning is that the secret of being happy is doing things for other people.*

DICK GREGORY

Too much of a good thing can be wonderful.

MAE WEST

No objects of value . . . are worth risking the priceless experience of waking up one more day.

— JACK SMITH

The best way out of a difficulty is through it.

ANONYMOUS

Life is a succession of moments. To live each one is to succeed.

CORITA KENT

Instead of allowing yourself to be so unhappy, just let your love grow as God wants it to grow; seek goodness in others, love more persons more; love them more impersonally, more unselfishly, without thought of return. The return, never fear, will take care of itself.

Henry Drummond

Do something. If it doesn't work, do something else. No idea is too crazy.

JIM HIGHTOWER

To love and be loved is to feel the sun from both sides.

DAVID VISCOTT

Live full today, and let no pleasure
pass untasted—
And no transient beauty scorn;
Fill well the storehouse of the soul's delight
With light of memory—
Who knows? Tomorrow may be—Night.

Anonymous

Strengthen me by sympathizing with my strength, not my weakness.

A. BRONSON ALCOTT

The only limit to our realization of tomorrow will be our doubts of today.

FRANKLIN D. ROOSEVELT

The biggest human temptation is . . . to settle for too little.

THOMAS MERTON

The tragedy of life doesn't lie in not reaching your goal. The tragedy lies in having no goal to reach.

— Benjamin E. Mays

God loves you. God doesn't want anyone to be hungry and oppressed. He just puts his big arms around everybody and hugs them up against himself.

Norman Vincent Peale

Let us go singing as far as we go: the road will be less tedious.

VIRGIL

> When it is dark enough,
> you can see the stars.

— CHARLES A. BEARD

Keep a green tree in your heart and perhaps the singing bird will come.

CHINESE PROVERB

To wish to be well is a part of becoming well.

SENECA

The thing always happens that you really believe in; and the belief in a thing makes it happen.

FRANK LLOYD WRIGHT

*Problems are
only opportunities
in work clothes.*

— Henry J. Kaiser

This book was typeset in Centaur MT and Savoye

by Nina Gaskin.

Cover and interior design

by Judith Stagnitto Abbate